Copper Beech Farm is a wonderful sight
Perched on a hill on the Isle of Wight.
To the west are some woodlands
To break up the wind.
To the east is a chapel
For those that have sinned.
To the north is the Solent
Where many yachts sail. To the south is a Mouse
That sells very fine Ale.

**Who Lives at
Copper Beech Farm?**

For more information contact:
Author: Rex Pho: dixieprickle@gmail.com

Illustrator & Designer: Claire S Bicknell: claire@stylographics.com
Bark • Linked in • @101illustrations • +44 7940 599 455

Published by: 101Illustrations

*Children aged 5 or 6 will
need adult support in
parts of this book*

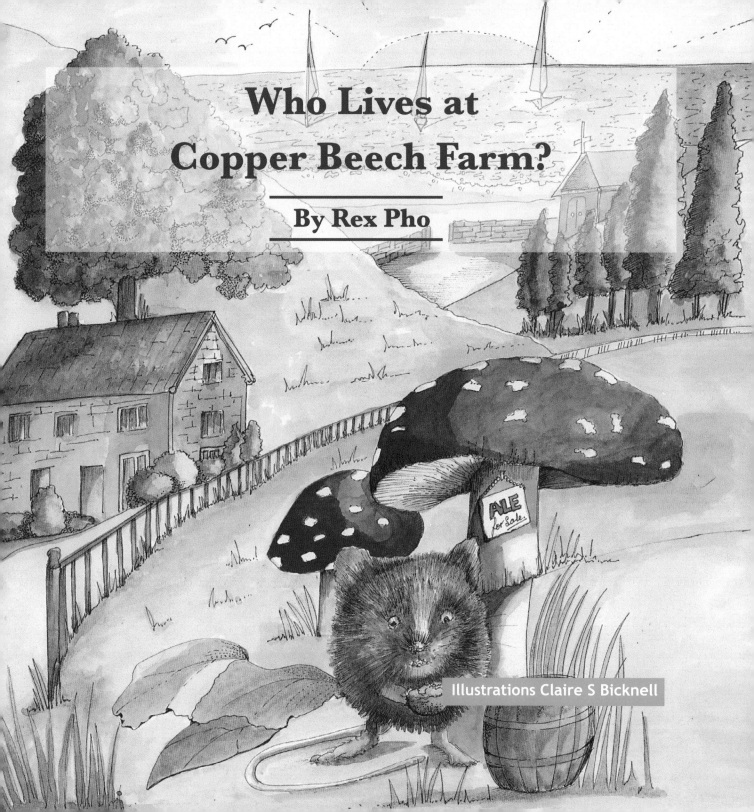

Who Lives at Copper Beech Farm?

By Rex Pho

ALE for Sale.

Illustrations Claire S Bicknell

Gilbert Prickle was
reclining on a bed of straw

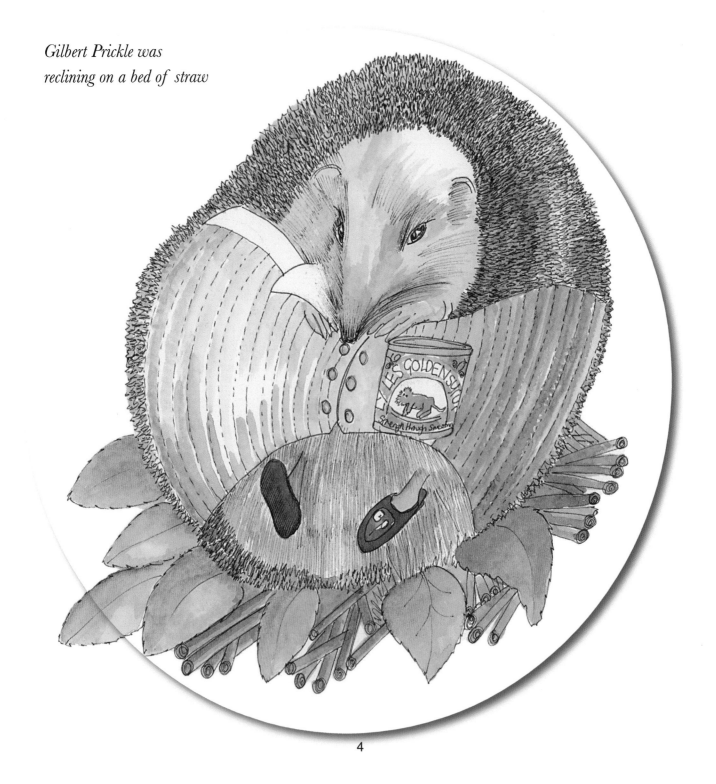

"Myrtle, call the boys. We have too many people in here and somebody must move out." Gilbert Prickle was reclining on a bed of straw, dressed in his fawn corduroy jacket with monogrammed silk slippers. In his left hand was a cup of what he called Plum Tea, which he made in an old Tate and Lyle syrup tin bearing a picture of a lion and the motto "Strength through Sweetness". Myrtle thought it was rather strong tea. If he had two cups of it on Christmas morning he was likely to go to sleep and wake up with a headache. Myrtle was the most beautiful hedgehog that Gilbert had ever seen. She had pink lips and perfect teeth, and her topknot was tied in a light blue ribbon. Best of all, she was very round, which among hedgehogs is a sign on of great beauty.

"Just ask the boys to come in – Albert, Schubert, Englebert and Hubert. Don't bother the girls or children". Englebert appeared first with his mop of black hair neatly brushed into a quiff. They heard him before they saw him, singing a ditty as usual.

"Bug'o me! Bug'o me!

Slug 'o me! Slug 'o me!

I've got the munchies

I'd like something crunchie

A slug on some toast would be fine!"

The Prickle family lived in a tangle of weeds and brambles woven around a pile of farmyard scrap iron. There were old ploughs and harrows, cast iron fences and the odd wheel and milk churn. They had chosen it because it was safe from badgers and nestled against the north wall of the pigsty. There was a brick missing from the pigsty wall, and they sometimes went through the hole to steal some piggy biscuits. These were very hard and they were frightened by Miss Mango, a vast hairy pink pig that lived in the sty. She was said to be very grumpy, so the Bert family avoided her when she was awake. They were known as the Berts because all the boy's names ended in Bert.

Englebert appeared first with his mop of black hair neatly brushed into a quiff. Schubert playing the penny whistle... Hubert was an odd mix of serious and dull and Albert was obsessed with dressing as a Ship's Captain!

"What's Up?" said Albert as he joined his family. Suddenly, they were bathed in sun light as the roof above them vanished. They all looked up in surprise, and dangling above them was little Dixie Prickle, hanging from a metal spike by the straps of his blue dungarees.

Doreen let out a cry, "Dixie! What are you doing up there? Come down at once!". Clearly this was not possible.

"Look Mummy. I can fly!" said Dixie, wiggling his arms and legs in pleasure.

A big brown hand appeared and lifted Dixie off his spike and lowered him back into the nest. A voice said "Take it easy Charlie. There's hoglets in here."

They all looked up in surprise, and dangling above them was little Dixie Prickle, hanging from a metal spike by the straps of his blue dungarees.

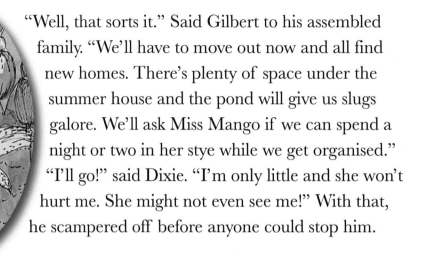

"Well, that sorts it." Said Gilbert to his assembled family. "We'll have to move out now and all find new homes. There's plenty of space under the summer house and the pond will give us slugs galore. We'll ask Miss Mango if we can spend a night or two in her stye while we get organised." "I'll go!" said Dixie. "I'm only little and she won't hurt me. She might not even see me!" With that, he scampered off before anyone could stop him.

When he poked his nose through the hole in the brick wall, he realised that he might have been a bit foolish. There, almost touching him, was a giant pair of hairy pink nostrils blowing bubbles of slime at him. "Oh! Are you Miss Mango? I have come to ask a favour, but I'm rather frightened of you."

"I'll go!" said Dixie to Doreen
"I'm only little and she won't hurt
me. She might not even see me!"

"No need, dear Boy" said the vast hairy pig, as the nostrils retreated. "We are all hogs together. You are just a small hog that lives in hedgerows, and I am a big hog that would like to live in a forest guzzling acorn. How does the farmer expect me to make good bacon on the slop that he feeds me? It's like boiled sawdust. I need apples and oats, potato and gravy, swedes and parsnips. Even the pig nuts that he gives me are tasteless. Oops! I am prone to moan and there was something you wanted. How can I help?"

"The farmer is clearing away our nest and we need shelter for a night or two while we find new homes."

"No problem! Make yourselves at home. Help yourselves to pig nuts. You might like them, but they are mighty hard." "But there are lots of us. More than a dozen. Are you sure?"

"Settle against the north wall and make yourselves comfy. I'm less likely to sit on you and squash you then."

Dixie recalled a story told by Grandpa Gilbert about his brother Wilfred Prickle who was sat on by Miss Mango's mother. Fortunately, the straw bedding was very deep, and Wilfred was able to wriggle free. But it gave him a nasty fright.

"Oh! Are you Miss Mango? I have come to ask a favour, but I'm rather frightened of you."

12

Dixie reported back through the hole in the wall that the coast was clear, and a family procession made its way into the sty. Led by Gilbert and Myrtle, it was followed by Albert and Doreen, Englebert and Kylie with little Lilly Prickle wrapped in a fur coat, Schubert and Chardonnay and Hubert with Anaglypta who was very young, and pale faced with lumpy skin.

"Phew! It certainly pongs of pig in here," said Kylie. "I'm not sure it's very healthy for Lilly. We'll make a nest near the missing brick, so that Lilly can have some fresh air."

After a restful day in their new nests, the boys set out to find some food. Word soon reached the women that something had been built on the site of their old nest. In the dark, nobody could make out what it was, so the matter was left until the morning.

"Word soon reached the women Doreen, Chardonnay, Kylie & Anaglypta that somthing had been built on the site of their old nest."

14

As Miss Mango opened her eyes, Kylie was letting off steam. "I've had it! Enough! This place stinks and it's filthy. There's nothing to eat and I'm moving out and taking Lilly Prickle with me. I'm not spending another night in this place! I need a wash!" She still had on her blue polka dot dress from yesterday, which was all crumpled with bits of straw poking out everywhere.

"Where will you go?" asked Dixie.

"I think we have a new home." said Hubert. "I've just been out to see a man about a slug and there are big tractor tyres where our old nest was. They have arches cut into the worn-out tread and we could build new nests in there. No badger would be able to get at us."

They decided that Hubert and Albert should go and explore the new structure to see if it was suitable.

"It's lovely," reported Albert. There are big tyres with connecting archways. The middle is full of straw, and there is a corrugated iron sheet on top to keep the rain out. We'd be very comfortable and there's room for all of us."

Kylie was letting off steam. "I've had it! Enough! This place stinks and it's filthy."

17

"Miss Mango, we are very grateful for your hospitality," said Gilbert. "Myrtle and I are taking the family off to our new home across the yard. We'll be gone by lunchtime but will pop in from time to time to say Hello."

After a while, Miss Mango heard rustling straw and hedgehog laughter, and realised that the Prickles were moving out. She wandered over to the hole in the wall to wave them goodbye, only to see the departing backside of Gilbert Prickle at the rear of the procession. She felt a little bit downcast because she had enjoyed having their company. This unhappy feeling did not last long. There, having been pushed through the hole in the brickwork, was a big red apple. She knew it was a thankyou from the Prickles and was so touched that little tears came to her piggy eyes.

"There, having been pushed through the hole in the brickwork, was a big red apple. She knew it was a thankyou from the Prickles"

It didn't take long for all the Berts to start gathering straw from the middle of the tyres to make new nests.

"Oi!" said a soft voice from the straw.

"What are you doing?"

"We are making new nests," said Hubert.

"Who are you?"

"I'm Thethil" said the voice as two faces appeared from the straw. The face that spoke had a very fine moustache. "And thith ith my wife Thithely."

"Don't mind him," said Cicely. He has a lisp and is sometimes a bit difficult to understand. His name is Cecil. We are slowworms - legless lizards"

"Snakes Alive!" exclaimed Schubert, who had a protective arm around Chardonnay. "I'm not sure that I like snakes. Don't you swallow your food whole?"

"Indeed we do. But mothly we eat thlugs and anyway we are not thnaketh. Our teeth point backwardth tho that the thlugth can't wiggle free. We thleep motht of the time and the thun on the corrugated iron keepth uth warm."

"Do you mind sharing your home with us?" asked Gilbert.

"We don't mind at all. We go out at dusk to get some food and come back before we get too cold. We need heat,

20

"Oi!" said a soft voice from the straw. "What are you doing?"

which is why we try to soak up the sun during the day. Isn't that right Cecil?."

"Yeth. We are good neighbourth and don't have partieth!"

Thus it was that the tyres became home to the Prickle family and two slowworms. They all spent the rest of the day getting their nests in good order and as it got dark, they went out in search of some supper.

They were watched by Nell, a retired Border Collie who was now too old to chase around after sheep. She roamed about Copper Beech Farm at will and had a large and comfortable kennel close to the kitchen door. She knew everything that went on in the farmyard and was always on watch for visitors whether friends or foe. She let out a low growl as Dixie approached. "Dixie, come and have some supper with me. I have something you will like." Dixie was quite taken aback to be invited to supper by Nell, who said, "I'll lay down for a moment, and you can climb along my tail and onto my shoulders. I'll carry you back to my kennel."

"I'll lay down for a moment, and you can climb along my tail and onto my shoulders said Nell to Dixie.

It was lovely and warm in the kennel with a thick bed of clean straw on the floor. Nell helped Dixie to slide off her back and she fetched an old biscuit tin from the back of her kennel. She prised the lid off with one paw and offered the tin to Dixie. "What are these please Nell?"

"Well, they are not really biscuits. They are made from dried liver and are very chewy. My teeth are not too good now that I am getting old, but you will have no problem with them."

Dixie reached into the tin and took out a black and leathery 'biscuit' about the size of a postage stamp. "Smells OK," he said as he bit into a corner with his sharp little teeth. "Ooh! That's tasty," he said. " Much nicer than slug but not as crispy as earwig."

"Put some in your pocket for later. Your mum might like to try one. Any time you want some more, just pop over. The farmer always keeps my tin topped up. Now. Have you ever seen a badger?"

Gilbert & Myrtle were madly in love!

"What! No, and I never want to. They eat hedgehogs and I'd be scared."

"I think you should see one so that you know what they look like. I know where they hunt in the evening and will take you there. You'll be safe with me. Hop up on my shoulders again, and we'll set out. Don't talk. Just whisper in my ear if you need to."

Nell walked quietly from the farmhouse and went past the barn where tractors were stored. Past the chicken sheds and the piggery and stopped when she came to the pond. "We'll hide here among the brambles. The badgers come here to look for worms and to have a drink. If we stay here, the wind will carry our scent away from the pond. They have poor eyesight but they are good at hearing and smelling."

They waited quietly and after about half-an-hour Dixie saw some movement in the moonlight. "Look! Is that them?" he whispered.

The animals were almost impossible to see in the gloom. They were little more than shadows. One of them made a noise like a cough.

"That's them! See how big they are. They are very strong."

Nell & Dixie watched the badgers

A shaft of moonlight lit up the badgers snuffling round the edge of the pond and one of them looked straight towards Nell and Dixie.

"It's OK Dixie. He can't see us and is just looking around to make sure that they are not in danger. See – he's gone back to searching for worms."

"Can we go now? I really don't like badgers. They frighten me and I don't want to be eaten for breakfast."

"I'll take you back to your new home," said Nell. We can snuggle down and wait for your parents to come home.

Sure enough, five minutes later Nell was laying down beside the tyres with Dixie nestling between her front legs. Dixie was completely covered by Nell's fur, and only his little face was visible beneath her chin as he dosed in complete comfort and security.

Dixie felt safe curled up next to Nell

He didn't dream of badgers, but of all the adventures that he could have with his new friend Nell. Today it was badgers. Maybe a bull tomorrow?

30

LIVING WITH YOUR HEDGEHOGS

Hedgehogs walk about a mile every night looking for food.
Help them get into and out of your garden by having holes
in walls or fences. These should be about the size of an open
adult hand.

They like to hide and will happily occupy piles of leaves,
twigs and logs. They like compost heaps and bonfires. Make
sure these are not occupied before you rake, dig or burn.

Ponds into which hedgehogs can fall
should have either a safe island or a
gently sloping beach.

Hedgehogs will eat many things, mostly
insects including beetles, worms, slugs,
baby mice and bird's eggs. They like
meaty things most, but in autumn they
will eat soft fruit as well. Don't offer them
bread and milk – it's not good for them.

The British Hedgehog Preservation Society website provides a lot of useful information.
Visit https://www.britishhedgehogs.org.uk/

The End...

Printed in Great Britain
by Amazon